Celebrating the next generation
of explorers—from their small
steps to their giant leaps.

THIS BOOK BELONGS TO

I was putting the finishing touches on my solar system model when the bell rang.

"Don't forget the science class bake sale tomorrow," called Mrs. Bunsen.

"The bake sale competition is here!" I squealed.

MRS. B'S
SCIENCE CLASS
BAKE
SALE

11am–3pm

HELP US GET A TELESCOPE !!!

"Not a competition, Luna Muna," corrected Mrs. Bunsen. "We're working together to raise money for a telescope that the entire class can enjoy!"

But I barely heard her. There are three things I love: space, baking, and contests. I was already imagining all the yummy ways I could win.

"It has to be something delicious," I told Mommy that night. "And out of this world!"

"How about your cupcakes?" suggested Mommy. "You could share a fun fact in each wrapper."

My cosmic cupcakes did check all the boxes. But would they be the best?

I wasn't certain. I'd have to make a final decision tomorrow.

The next day, preparation for the science bake sale was in full swing.

Aaron helped Ashley dip ripe strawberries in
chocolate to make ladybugs. I learned that
their bright red color warns away predators.

Poppy and Greg were decorating a Jell-O ocean. They explained that more than eighty percent of our ocean is still unexplored.

Meena sprinkled sugar on mini volcano muffins. I learned that the hot liquid inside a volcano is called magma.

I saw a dinosaur cake, chemistry cookies, Rice Krispie robots, pretzel stick thermometers, and even a giant ice cream sundae with beakers full of toppings.

FUNDS RAISED!

ICECREAM

BAKE SALE!
11 AM - 3 PM

Everyone was working together to prepare something scientifically delicious.

"I can't wait to see what you brought, Luna Muna!" said Mrs. Bunsen.

"Always save the best for last!" I said.

"It's not a contest," reminded Mrs. Bunsen.

Just then, an idea hit me. It was my best one ever.

Why choose just one space treat when I could open an entire space café full of lots of different desserts?

People would be amazed! They would learn about the entire universe!

I put up a sign and got to work.

"Do you need help, Luna Muna?" asked Poppy.

"Thanks, but I can do it all by myself," I called back.

I would start with cosmic cupcakes and planetary cake pops, and then move on to black hole brownies, lunar lollipops, and constellation cookies.

And that was only the beginning! I pictured a
galactic swirl of the yummiest treats in the universe.

LUNA MUNA'S
SPACE CAFÉ

MENU
★ Cosmic Cupcakes...... $3
★ Planetary Pops........ $2
★ Black Hole Brownies.... $3
★ Constellation Cookies...... $2
★ Lunar Lollipops.......... $1
★ Seismic Mooncakes...... $3

This would be the best Space Café my school had ever seen. In fact, I would open this café in space one day, too!

I put on my special space helmet and began to float around like the amazing astronaut baker I was.

"Three...Two...One...

Bake sale blast off!"

I whispered to myself.

I floated back and forth, grabbing everything I needed. I was mixing, pouring, balancing, and baking. And I was doing it all at record speed.

"Be careful, Luna Muna!" said Greg.

"Everything is under control!" I called down. "I'm just a baker on a mission!" I moved faster and faster. Everything was a blur.

Too fast! I spun into the table and watched as all my hard work exploded into a cloud of flour and sugar. Globs of icing clung to my hair. Batter and sprinkles covered the floor. My cake pops were cake plops.

It was one gigantic, galactic mess. Tears sprung to my eyes. "Houston, we have a problem..." I said to myself.

"We can help, Luna Muna!"
said Poppy.
"We're a team!" said Greg.

"How? Everything is ruined," I cried.
"Now no one will learn about space."
Aaron and Ashley helped me up.
"I have an idea…" said Meena.

Soon we had a plan.
"3...2...1.... BAKE SALE BLASTOFF!" we yelled.

FUNDS RAISED!

Bake sale today!

HELP US BUY A CLASS TELESCOPE!

SPACE EXPLORER

We scrubbed and swept and mopped and wiped.
We iced and sprinkled and rolled and shaped.
Everything looked space-tastic...even better than I had imagined!

We finished just in time.
A big group of hungry-looking
customers was heading our way.

Aaron and Ashley took orders while
Meena retrieved them. Poppy packaged
the treats and Greg collected the money.
I shared fun space facts with all the
customers. It was a perfect system.

We were more than a team.
We were a crew.

"These muffins are out of this world," said one customer.

"I didn't know that Mars had the biggest volcano in the solar system!"

"These pretzels are from another planet!" exclaimed a third.

"And this must be the best Jell-O in the universe," said another.

"I wonder if there's life on Jupiter's ocean moon Europa?"

"Did you know that Venus is the hottest planet in our solar system?"

My cheeks hurt from smiling.

I talked about how an asteroid impact spelled the end of the dinosaurs, how robots help us explore other planets, and even how NASA once sent ladybugs to space!

We held our breath while Meena emptied the money jar and counted it all up. It was exactly enough for the telescope!

"Congratulations, everyone!" said Mrs. Bunsen.
"That was the best bake sale I've ever seen!"

"Mission accomplished!" I cheered.
"But it's not a competition."
Everyone laughed.

Space is everywhere. It's our shared past and our shared future. I still plan to open a real space café one day, but I know I won't be doing it alone. In the meantime, my whole class can explore space together with our new telescope.

Luna's Cosmic Cupcakes

1/2 cup unsalted butter, softened
1/2 cup white sugar
2 large eggs
2 teaspoons vanilla extract
1/2 cup milk of choice

1 1/4 cups all-purpose flour
1 1/4 teaspoons baking powder
1/4 teaspoon salt

1. Preheat the oven to 350 degrees F and line a muffin tin with cupcake liners.
2. Add the butter and sugar to a medium bowl. Beat with an electric mixer until light and fluffy (3-5 min). Add in the eggs and vanilla and mix until combined.
3. Add the baking powder, salt, and half of the flour to the bowl. Beat on low speed. Add half of the milk. Beat again on low. Add the remaining flour and milk and beat on low until fully combined.
4. Fill each cupcake liner with about ¼ cup batter.
5. Bake for 20-22 minutes. Remove from the oven and transfer cupcakes to a wire rack and let cool completely.
6. Frost as desired, and add sprinkles, of course!

Did You Know?

The famous freeze-dried "Astronaut Ice Cream" was served only once in space, on Apollo 7 in 1968! It was too crumbly and astronauts didn't love the taste. But decades later, when Space Shuttle Atlantis carried a science freezer to the International Space Station in 2006, NASA took the opportunity to send real ice cream to space for the first time!

Galactic Cupcake Toppers

1.

1. Cut stars and circles out of construction paper.
2. Use your imagination and decorate the shapes using crayons, markers, paint, sequins, etc.
3. Add a thin line of glue onto the back of each shape, and place the top half of a toothpick onto the glue.
4. Once dry, place the toothpick into the cupcake for a galactic decoration!

2.

3.

GLUE

4.

Published by DragonFruit, an imprint of Mango Publishing Group, a division of Mango Media.

Cover, illustration, and layout design: Allyson Wilson

Luna Muna: Space Cafe.

Library of Congress Cataloging-in-Publication number: 2023939871

ISBN:
(print) 978-1-68481-237-0
(ebook) 978-1-68481-238-7

BISAC category code: JUV036010, JUVENILE FICTION / Technology / Astronauts & Space

Printed in China.

AUTHOR

Kellie Gerardi is an aerospace and technology professional, a popular science communicator, and a commercial astronaut flying to space on a dedicated research mission with Virgin Galactic. Kellie lives in Jupiter, Florida, with her husband and their daughter Delta V. You can follow her adventures on social media: @kelliegerardi

ILLUSTRATOR

Allyson Wilson is a graphic designer and illustrator who works on children's books, greeting cards, home decor, and more! She lives in Pennsylvania with her husband, Josh, and two shining stars, Felicity and Elliott. You can follow her on Instagram: @Allyson.Wilson_Art

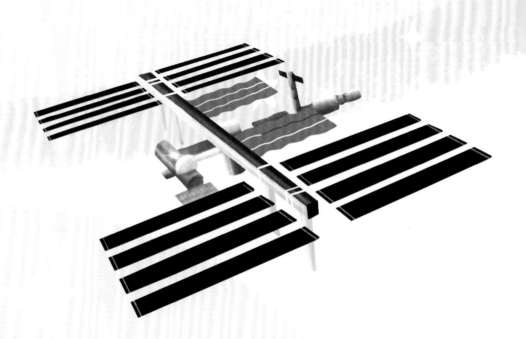

Luna Muna has been to space!
A copy of *Luna Muna* was flown to the
International Space Station in 2023 with
the Axiom-2 crew. Commander
Peggy Whitson read the story
aloud from space as part of the
crew's STEM outreach initiatives to
inspire children around the world.

Praise for the LUNA MUNA series!

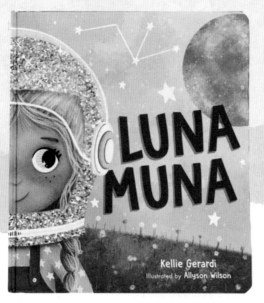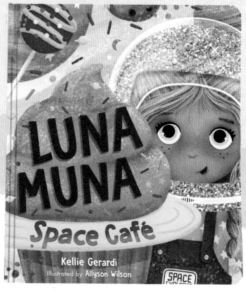

"The perfect book for aspiring astronauts!"

"Imaginative, sparkly, and fun!"

"A joy to read."

Stay tuned for Luna Muna's next adventure, coming in 2024!

DragonFruit, an imprint of Mango Publishing, publishes high-quality children's books to inspire a love of lifelong learning in readers. DragonFruit publishes a variety of titles for kids, including children's picture books, nonfiction series, toddler activity books, pre-K activity books, science and education titles, and ABC books. Beautiful and engaging, our books celebrate diversity, spark curiosity, and capture the imaginations of parents and children alike. You can follow @DragonFruitKids on Instagram and @MangoPublishing on Twitter.